Mona Lisa

THE SECRET OF THE SMILE

LETIZIA GALLI

Translated by

NICHOLAS B. A. NICHOLSON

A DOUBLEDAY BOOK FOR YOUNG READERS

TO ANTONIO, POET, SCIENTIST, CHILD.

The water you touch in a river is the last of that which has passed
and the first of that which is coming. Thus it is with time present.

Notebooks. Morals 1174

A Doubleday Book for Young Readers

Published by
Delacorte Press
Bantam Doubleday Dell Publishing Group, Inc.
1540 Broadway
New York, NY 10036

Doubleday and the portrait of an anchor with a dolphin are trademarks
of Bantam Doubleday Dell Publishing Group, Inc.

Illustrations and English translation copyright © 1996 by Letizia Galli

Library of Congress Cataloging-in-Publication Data

Galli, Letizia.
    Mona Lisa : the secret of the smile / by Letizia Galli.
        p.   cm.
    ISBN 0-385-32108-2
    1. Leonardo, da Vinci, 1452-1519—Juvenile literature. 2. Painters—Italy—
Biography—Juvenile literature. 3. Leonardo, da Vinci, 1452-1519. Mona
Lisa—Juvenile literature. [1. Leonardo, da Vinci, 1452-1519. 2. Artists. 3.
Leonardo, da Vinci, 1452-1519. Mona Lisa.] I. Leonardo, da Vinci, 1452-
1519. II. Title.
ND623.L5G32   1996
759.5—dc20   94-35416   CIP   AC

The photograph of the Mona Lisa on page 30 was provided by
Scala/Art Resource, New York.
The text of this book is set in 15-point Janson Text.
Manufactured in Italy
March 1996
10 9 8 7 6 5 4 3 2 1

The most famous smile in the world belongs to the woman called Mona Lisa. Five hundred years ago, her mysterious smile was painted by Leonardo da Vinci, an artist who always looked for answers to the unanswerable.

When Leonardo da Vinci was a little boy, he was full of curiosity. He invented strange riddles that made his friends laugh, and he asked questions that stunned his teachers.

"Why does water flow?" he asked.

"Why do the birds fly?" he challenged.

"Why can't plants walk?" he demanded.

The teachers' faces turned red. They had no idea how to respond.

"Patience," thought Leonardo. "One day I will understand these mysterious things."

One day Leonardo's teacher said to the class, "Today we practice handwriting." The students wrote very carefully. But when he saw Leonardo's paper, the teacher exclaimed, "Leonardo, this is impossible to read!" "Nothing is impossible!" Leonardo replied, and held up a mirror. Now the writing could be read perfectly. Leonardo had written backward for the first time and would continue writing backward forever.

E ven after he grew up, Leonardo continued to amaze people. Rich people wore expensive clothes made of precious silk that trailed to the floor. They were very beautiful, but so uncomfortable! Leonardo had his tailor make him short, simple clothes in bright colors. People stared and wondered why he dressed so oddly.

"The truth," said Leonardo with a secretive smile, "is that these clothes are the most comfortable."

People thought Leonardo was odd for other reasons. Leonardo was a vegetarian, but he still went to the market and bought sparrows, pigeons, and quail. "What does he do with them?" everyone wondered. Leonardo took the birds home and set them free. He watched them fly away and drew them, hoping to discover the secret of flight.

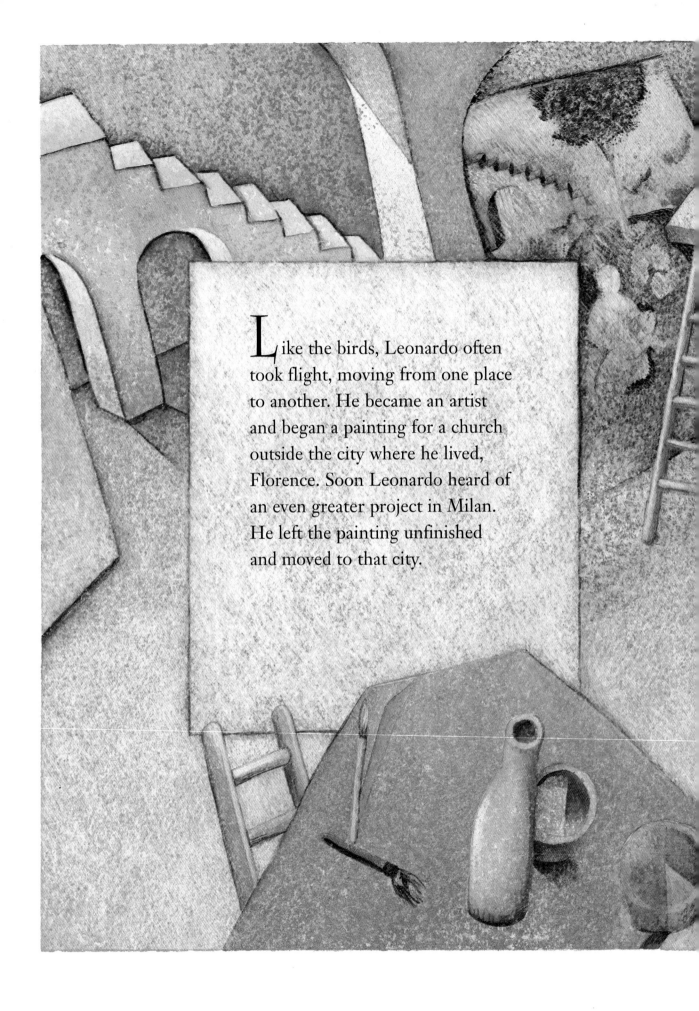

Like the birds, Leonardo often
took flight, moving from one place
to another. He became an artist
and began a painting for a church
outside the city where he lived,
Florence. Soon Leonardo heard of
an even greater project in Milan.
He left the painting unfinished
and moved to that city.

The Duke of Milan, the city's ruler, wanted to build a statue of his father on horseback. It was to be the largest statue in the world. Only Leonardo was capable of discovering how to create such a masterpiece.

But masterpieces are hard work. It took Leonardo years to figure out how to make the enormous sculpture, and even longer to find the right horse to use as a model! Although Leonardo did many studies of the horse, he never finished the statue.

In fact, one reason Leonardo never finished the sculpture was because the Duke kept him so busy. When the Duke wanted celebrations for royal weddings, whom did he call? Leonardo, of course! Leonardo designed fantastic costumes, moving stages, and fireworks. Leonardo's festivals were the talk of Europe, and everyone wanted to attend them.

Everyone also wanted Leonardo to paint their portraits. Leonardo made women appear young and beautiful. But Leonardo wanted to do more than plan festivals and paint ladies of the court. He still had many questions, and he wrote them down—backward, of course!

You must discover the secret of lightning, and why tears flow—what the moon is made of and where it goes. . .

Leonardo da Vinci also wanted to invent things that would make everyday life more comfortable. He wanted to know how he could make warm water run from faucets, and how people could swim without drowning. As Leonardo looked for answers to these amazing questions, his notebooks filled with drawings for inventions that looked like bicycles, helicopters, and parachutes— hundreds of years before they actually existed. But that was not all.

Leonardo still studied birds, hoping to discover the secret of flight. He sketched and wrote backward in his notebooks. One day he built a flying machine of canvas and wood that was powered by one man. The man leapt from a tall tower, but the machine crashed, and the man in it was badly bumped and bruised. "Hmmm," said Leonardo, "I'll have to work on this."

Leonardo had a lot of work to do in Milan. He had paintings to plan, the largest sculpture in the world to finish, and dozens of experiments to carry out. But when he heard that the city of Florence was looking for an artist to paint a huge battle scene on the largest wall of the biggest room in the greatest palace in the city, Leonardo went home.

And when he arrived, Leonardo knew just how to create the painting. "You'll need mobile scaffolding, a special glue to hold the colors, and a special stove to dry the glue and the colors," he wrote. But suddenly a terrible flood came, and the scaffolding, paints, and stove were swept away. Unfortunately, so was the painting of the great Battle of Anghiari. But Leonardo had already found his next challenge. What could it be?

Leonardo had met a woman called Mona Lisa. She was very kind and had a magical smile. Enchanted, Leonardo began to mix his colors. "What are you going to do, maestro?" she asked. Leonardo studied her as he had studied the water, the wind, and the birds. "I'm going to paint exactly what I see," he replied mysteriously.

Leonardo had planned the world's largest sculpture. He had created the greatest festivals ever seen. He had worked toward inventions that were centuries ahead of his time.

When he painted Mona Lisa's portrait, Leonardo did something that had never been done before—he painted what he saw. And by capturing the magical smile of Mona Lisa, he turned it into the most famous smile in the world.

SOME NOTES ON LEONARDO DA VINCI

The Renaissance began in Italy and lasted from about 1500 to 1700. It was a time of great change and learning that produced many well-known rulers, writers, thinkers, and artists. The most famous of all Renaissance men and women is probably Leonardo da Vinci.

Leonardo was born in the small Italian town of Vinci in 1452. His name means "Leonardo from Vinci." His parents were not married to each other, and Leonardo grew up in his father's house. When Leonardo was fourteen, his father apprenticed him to an artist named Andrea del Verrocchio in Florence, which was the closest large city. Leonardo quickly became famous as an artist and began work on a large painting called *The Adoration of the Magi* for the church of San Donato at Scopeto, just outside Florence. Although Leonardo never finished this painting, the parts that he did complete, as well as many studies for the painting, can be seen today in Florence, in the museum called the Uffizi.

In 1482, Leonardo moved to the city of Milan and persuaded Ludovico Sforza (also known as Ludovico Il Moro), the Duke of Milan, to employ him. Leonardo stayed there until 1499, when Milan was captured by French invaders.

The first work Leonardo painted in Milan is the *Virgin of the Rocks*. There are actually two versions of this painting, one in the Louvre museum in Paris and another in the National Gallery in London.

The Last Supper is the most famous masterpiece Leonardo created in Milan. It was painted directly on the wall of a chapel in the church of Santa Maria delle Grazie in Milan. Although it is now in poor condition, one can see what remains of the painting there today.

Only studies of the Sforza monument—the statue of Francesco Sforza on horseback commissioned by his son, the Duke of Milan—have survived. In 1498, a clay model was completed, but it was destroyed after the French troops conquered Milan.

After leaving Milan, Leonardo traveled around Italy, staying in many cities for short periods. In Florence, he painted the famous Mona Lisa. He kept this painting for himself and carried it with him when he moved to France in 1516, where he had been invited by King Francis I. Leonardo died in France in 1519. The Mona Lisa now hangs in the Louvre in Paris.

Throughout his life, Leonardo recorded his ideas in notebooks. Thousands of pages of his drawings, records of experiments, observations, and plans still exist today. They were all written backward, from right to left. These notebooks reveal the true genius of Leonardo da Vinci.

In them one can see that Leonardo learned more about anatomy than anyone else had ever known by dissecting people and animals and drawing what he found. He drew fantastic machines that resembled submarines, tanks, and helicopters, long before anyone else had ever imagined such things. He drew magnificent buildings that were never built and conducted many scientific experiments. He studied mathematics, medicine, botany, and many other subjects. More than any other person, Leonardo da Vinci represents the spirit of the Renaissance.